Dedicated to the special littles that I love in my life!
Christian Campbell
Ericsson Industrious
Riley Campbell
Tristyn Johnson
David Hill
In memory of my beloved grandmother, Catherine Sneed, my father, David Argrow and Christian's paternal grandmother, Veronica Campbell.

"Life happens as it will and as it should. Dreams deferred come back to us at their intended times."

K. E. Argrow

Contents

Preface

I embarked on the journey of writing Marley McGee the Majestic with the intent to help young scholars to always remember you are wonderful, brilliant, and there is NO ONE else in the world like you! Only you can be you! Isn't that magnificent? How amazingly unique you are!

It is my hope, that while reading this enchanting novel, you find your inner strength as Marley finds his inner powers to face dark forces.

Happy Learning!

K. E. Argrow

Acknowledgement

There are so many people in my life who made writing this book possible. If I don't mention you, it doesn't mean that you aren't important to me because you are. Know that if you love me, I love you too.

I would first like to thank my son Christian Liam Campbell for inspiring me to write this book. Your birth is the best thing that has ever happened to me. You always provide light on my darkest days. It's not your responsibility to do so, but your presence is so inspiring. You are my why. I want Christian and every other child to see through Marley that they are great in every instance, whether they were raised in a single parent household or whether they were raised in a castle by a king and queen. Your greatness comes from within.

I would next like to thank my mother, Sarahlyn Phillips. There are not enough words to express all that you are to me. You are the reason that I am here. I say this not because you gave birth to me, but because you provided me with strength and kept me going at times that I wanted to give up. It is my goal to take care of you as you have taken care of myself and my beloved siblings. Thank you to my bonus father, Howard Phillips, for your endless encouragement and support and for loving my mother.

Thank you to Leighton Campbell for making me a parent and blessing me with my most precious gift. We are forever bonded. I'll always love you.

Thank you to the fabulous four —Dayavona Ward, Daysha Argrow-Hill and her spouse, Bobby Hill, Catherine Argrow-Cummings, and Daveeda Argrow —my sisters who have been my friends from day one. Thank you for encouraging and supporting me. Thank you for counseling and correcting me when needed.

Thank you to my nieces and nephews, Ronnie Harden III, Sarahlyn Argrow, Taylor Ward, Robyn Cummings, Keaytlin Ward, Willow Ward, Ericsson Industrious, Tristyn Johnson, and David Hill. You all are so wonderful. Know that you were a major inspiration for me writing this book. I want the best for you all, and I want to help provide that for you.

Thank you to *all of my* family and friends.

Thank you to all of my teachers who contributed to my education. You likely won't find this undertaking without errors, but I think you'd be proud of my work.

Thank you to the US Army for my experiences! Army strong! Hooah!

Thank you to everyone who contributed to the completion of this book. Thank you to all who believed in me. You know who you are.

Best,

K.E. Argrow

I

Marley McGee

the Majestic

K. E. Argrow

1

Chapter 1: He Always Knew

Even as the littlest of boys, Marley McGee would gaze out of any window that he came across in awe. It only made sense that one of Marley's first words was *door*, as he always wanted to play outside. At one and a half years old, Marley would grab his mother's hand and repeat the word *door* as he led her there. Once outside, Marley's hazel eyes would find their way to the big blue sky. Marley took a special interest in birds. "Wook, wook, wook!" he would shout with excitement whenever he saw a bird in flight. *Wook* was little Marley's word for *look*. Marley seemed to love the birds' freedom and adventurousness. His fascination for adventure would stay with him as he grew older. Marley always felt that there was something greater out there in the world. He always knew that there was more to life than his bright eyes could see.

"Marley McGee!"

"Yes, Mom?" Marley snapped back from his daydream, pulling himself away from staring out of the living room window. He wondered what he had done this time. Did he forget to wash the dishes? Did he not take the trash out? Did his mom play investigator and read his journal again? Marley knew that when his mother called him by his first and last names that he was going to be lectured about something.

Marley's mom walked into the living room. "Your teacher called. She' s concerned about you. Is there anything that you would like to talk to me about, son?"

"No, ma'am, I'm fine," Marley said.

But he was not at all fine. Marley and his mother had recently moved across the country for her new job. Marley missed his friends and hated the fact that he had to make new ones. What made matters worse is that they now lived in a house that they had inherited from Marley's grandfather. Marley despised the house. The house was huge, but he thought it was old, rickety, and just plain creepy. Little did he know what this shell of a house would have in store for him in the near future.

"Okay, son. Well, please let me know if you ever need to talk about anything, love. I love you, baby boy!"

"I love you too, Mom."

Marley hugged his mom and gave her a kiss on the cheek before going to his bedroom for the night. Marley and his mom had a very close relationship. It had been only the two of them living together since the day he came home from the hospital after he was born. Marley could talk to his mom about almost anything. There was one subject, though, that Marley didn't feel comfortable talking about with his mom. That one subject was his dad.

The absence of Marley's father was really beginning to bother him. This was the most significant reason why Marley's teacher noticed a change in him in school. Marley would see other children with their dads, and it hurt him that his was not there for him. He felt that he was missing out on so much. He wondered what his life would be like if he had a father to care for him, to play sports with him, to take him places, and just to be there with him every day. Marley knew that his mom was doing the best that she could to provide for him. He was very grateful for all that she did for him, but he couldn't help but feel as though he was missing out on so much because he didn't have a father. Marley often felt alone when his mom had to work long hours each day. He didn't want to hurt his mom, so he kept his feelings to himself. That night, Marley eventually fell asleep to escape his thoughts.

2

Chapter 2: Humdrum Break

It was Marley's last day of school before summer break and he was in his final class for the day waiting for the bell to ring.

"Class," said Mrs. Blankenship, Marley's teacher. "We have a few more minutes before the bell rings, and we won't see each other for some time. Does anyone care to share what activities they have planned for this summer break?"

Marley's classmates eagerly raised their hands to tell of their plans. One by one the students shared that they were going on amazing family vacations. Marley did not raise his hand. He had no plans for the summer. He knew that the most excitement he would have for the summer was watching television with his grandmother. Marley's mother had to work the entire summer, so she asked Marley's grandmother to come to their house to keep an eye on him while she was gone during the day.

Mrs. Blankenship noticed Marley did not raise his hand.

"Marley," she said. "What do you have planned for this summ—?"

The bell rang before Mrs. Blankenship could finish her

question. Marley was glad he didn't have to say anything. He didn't want to have to make up a trip he knew he was never going to take.

"Have an amazing summer, class. Stay safe. I will miss you guys," said Mrs. B.

The students all stood up from their seats and rushed to the door ready to begin their summer break. Marley left, too, and went to his bus line. Once on the bus, Marley took a seat at the front, sitting closest to the window. He stared out the bus window, thinking of how the other students had such fun vacations planned and he didn't. Marley soon fell asleep. The trip to his home from school was a long one. His bus driver, who the students all affectionately called Ms. D, shouted to wake him up when they arrived to his stop.

"M. McGee!"

Marley was startled out of his sleep.

"You fell asleep, young man! Be sure to enjoy your summer!"

"Thank you, Ms. D," Marley said as he exited the bus .

Marley walked into his house and saw his grandmother there waiting for him.

"Hey, Marley, how was your day, baby?"

"It was good, Granny."

Marley lovingly called his grandmother *Granny*. Marley's grandmother was there to make sure that he got home from school safely each day. His mother normally didn't get home from work until late, and Marley was too young to be home alone. Marley loved his granny very much, but he wondered why he needed a babysitter. He thought that he was too old to still have a babysitter, even if it was his granny.

"Today was your last day of school. Are you excited about your summer break, dear?"

"Yes, ma'am. I guess so." Marley wondered what there was for him to be excited about, but he knew not to disrespect his grandmother.

"I made you something to eat. It's on the table. You can grab whatever you want to drink from the refrigerator, baby. I wanted your drink to be cold. I also made you some cookies from scratch. I just took them out of the oven, so they' re still warm. I love you!"

"Thank you, Granny. I love you too!"

Marley quickly devoured his food. He was a growing boy, and he always worked up an appetite by the end of the school day.

"Thank you again, Granny. I'm going to my room to lie down. I'm tired."

"Okay, baby, your mom should be home shortly."

"Yes, ma'am."

Marley went to his bedroom, dropped his backpack on the floor, and plopped down on his bed fully dressed. He was exhausted and, right away, fell asleep.

3

Chapter 3: Whispers

Marley awoke the next morning excited that he had no school that day or the next day or the next. His smile quickly faded when he realized he had absolutely nothing to do. He got out of bed, showered, and brushed his teeth just to go plop on the couch and watch television. Marley yawned as he flipped through the channels. He quickly became bored and decided to eat breakfast before he got dressed and went outside.

Marley's house was old, but the amazing thing about it was that it was on *a lot of land*. There were many large trees on the land. One tree had a swing on it. The swing was made of an old tire and rope. Marley thought he'd give the swing a try for the first time. He swung back and forth, around and around. Marley's half smile turned into laughter with each kick that took him higher into the air as if he were flying. He swung until he got too dizzy to swing anymore. Then Marley got off the swing, and he began to explore.

Marley picked up a large stick and swung it back and forth as though he were a knight in a sword fight. Marley was an only child, so he was used to finding ways to amuse himself. He walked until he came upon a pond. Marley threw his stick down and grabbed a handful of rocks. He skipped the rocks on the pond until he noticed two birds playing. He watched the birds as he had since he was a little tot. Suddenly the birds began to take off in flight. Marley picked up his stick and began to run trying to keep up with them. Marley ran so fast that he felt as though he could leave the ground and fly alongside the birds. He stretched his arms out like he had wings and ran after the birds imitating their movements. The birds stopped and perched in a tree near Marley's house. Marley sat down with his back against the tree.

Exhausted, Marley's eyelids began to feel heavy. The sun shined on his face causing him to squint . He could hear windchimes as the wind blew. Marley closed his eyes.

"Marley," a voice whispered.

Marley barely opened his eyes; the sun was bright and shining directly in his face.

"Marley." The voice was louder.

He turned his head to look, but no one was there.

"Son!" the voice called out.

Marley awakened, startled that he was drenched in rain. It was storming outside. Marley realized that he had fallen asleep, and that for a short while, he had been dreaming.

He ran to his house where Granny greeted him at the door.

"Marley, baby, what were you doing out there?" she said. "Take your shoes off here and go get showered. Dinner is ready."

Marley showered and ate dinner alone at the table. His mom was still not home from work, and it was Granny's custom to always eat last. When he had finished eating dinner, as always, Marley kissed his granny on the cheek before going to his room for the night.

Marley lay on his bed and closed his eyes. Then, all of a sudden, he heard noises in his closet.

4

Chapter 4: The Box

"Ugh, this house is just plain creepy," Marley said, still lying down. "I can't wait to move from here. I'm over this place."

Marley closed his eyes again. The noise coming from his closet grew louder, and Marley noticed a light shining through the bottom of the door. Marley was startled.

"Now," he said. "I know I don't remember there being a light in that closet. Or was there? Oh well, I guess this comes along with the creepy territory."

Marley rolled over and, again, put his night mask on and closed his eyes. Marley was almost asleep, when he heard a whisper.

"Marley." Then the voice again whispered, "Marley."

Marley thought he must be dreaming, so he ignored the voice.

"*Son!*" the voice from earlier shouted, and he heard a crash in the closet.

Now Marley was scared. He grabbed his soccer trophy from his nightstand and tip toed over to his closet. Trembling, Marley snatched the door open with his trophy raised in the air just in case something unimaginable popped out at him. Oddly enough the light was gone. No one was in the closet; but there was a jewelry box on the ground. It appeared to have fallen from the closet's top shelf. Marley sat the trophy down and picked up the jewelry box. The box was locked. Marley wanted to know what was in the box, and so he tried his best to open it. He sat down in the closet, examined the box, and tried to pull it open without success.

Marley turned the box over. On its bottom was a message that read "You Have All That You Need." Marley read the message to himself over and over. He had no idea what the message meant. He looked at the shape of the lock on the jewelry box and wondered why it looked familiar. Marley sat there for some time staring at the box. He began to nod off and murmured with his head hanging, "My necklace."

Marley lifted his head, and half- awake, he grabbed his necklace that his grandfather had given him before he had passed. The necklace was golden with a half of a lion head pendant attached. Marley realized why the lock looked so familiar to him. He placed the pendant in the lock and slowly turned it. The box opened.

5

Chapter 5: Light in the Dark

Inside the box, to Marley's surprise, was the other half of the lion head pendant. Marley removed the pendant half from the box and put it together with the half on his necklace. It fit perfectly. Marley closed the jewelry box and placed it back on the top shelf of the closet. As he turned to leave the closet, he noticed the light from earlier. Marley turned around and saw a door with light shining through its cracks at the back of the closet. He was astonished. The young lad knew that this door was not there before.

He was scared, but he grabbed his now whole pendant and slowly, yet bravely walked toward the illuminated door. As Marley approached the door, he took a deep breath and grabbed the handle. He turned the handle and slowly pulled the door open. All that he could see was a blinding light. Marley quickly turned his head away and placed his arm over his face to block the bright light. As Marley turned his head back to face the light, with his arm still over his face, he looked into the door to see what was inside. Marley picked up a shoe and threw it into the door to see what would happen. Nothing happened, so Marley stepped closer to the door, still peering inside. Suddenly, he felt a tugging. Marley tried to turn away, but a strong force was pulling him inside the door. He tried and tried to break the hold, but there was nothing he could do to stop what was happening.

"Granny!" Marley screamed.

The door slammed shut, the light was gone, and so was Marley.

6

Chapter 6: It Was Just a Dream

Gasp!

Marley woke up in a panic. He sighed with relief and smiled a little when he realized he was in bed. But then he quickly realized he couldn't see anything. He felt his face.

"I still have this night mask on."

As Marley moved to remove the mask, he felt something wet and sticky on his feet.

"What is that? Is that a dog licking my feet? Um, but we don't have a dog . . ." Marley now rushed to take the mask from his face. "Agggghhhhhhhhhhhhh, aghhhhhhhhhhhh, aghhhhhhhhh!" Marley screamed. He was terrified by what he saw. "Aggghhhhhhh! Somebody help me! Mommaaaaa! Where am I? Somebody help me! Help me!"

Marley's door opened, and in rushed a young boy with dark skin and his hair in locks like Marley's. "Marley? What is wrong with you?"

"What do you mean what is wrong with me? Do you not see that over there, and who are you? Better yet where in the world am I?"

"Okay, Marley, this is not at all funny."

"You're telling me?" Marley asked the boy.

"Brother, I don't know what game you are playing, but I am going back to my chamber."

"No, please don't leave me here with that thing, and I don't have a brother. Where am I?""Okay, so I don't know if you hit your head or what, but I'll play along with you. As of late, I've been quite bored, so I'll oblige your need for theatrics. My name is David Sebastian. I am your older brother. You are in *your* chamber in our father's, the king's, castle. What's more, the *thing* you keep referring to is *your* pet Judah. Come and find me when your thoughts are in order."

David Sebastian left Marley with Judah.

Marley sat very still on his bed staring at Judah. Judah sat at the bottom of Marley's bed looking back at him. Marley was afraid to move, and rightfully so. Judah wasn't your ordinary pet. Judah was, in fact, a white lion with wings and eyes like embers of flames.

Marley gulped, closed his eyes, and lay back down. "Okay, this is a dream. I'm going to wake up soon," he said. Marley lay there for a while, then slowly opened his eyes. Judah was still there. "Okay, maybe if I put this back over my eyes. Yes, that's it." Marley put the night mask back on and again closed his eyes. He whispered , "Please wake up, please wake up, please wake up."

He lay there for a moment after his recitation. Marley then lifted a bit of the mask and peeked out to find that Judah was no longer at the foot of the bed. Marley sat up, removed the covers, and took the mask off with a sigh of relief; but it wasn't long before Marley felt as though a gaze was fixed upon him. His instinct led him to turn his head. Intuition is powerful. Sure enough, there Judah was on the side of the bed with his head resting on it.

A surprised Marley rolled out of the bed and fell onto the floor with a loud thud. Judah lifted his head from the bed to see what had happened to Marley. Marley got up just enough from the opposite side of the bed to peek over to get a good look at the mythical creature. It wasn't long before Marley realized Judah was mild-mannered.

"Why do you seem so familiar?" Marley hesitantly asked Judah as he looked into his eyes with a puzzled look on his face. After a few moments, which seemed like forever to Marley, Marley looked down at his pendant and realized that Judah resembled the lion on his charm. Marley slowly got back on the bed. He cautiously reached his hand out and petted Judah's head. Judah laid his head back on the bed and closed his eyes in approval.

7

Chapter 7: Leaders Serve

"Grab your armor and head to the chow hall. Grab your armor and head to the chow hall," a calm, almost robotic woman's voice called out over an intercom system.David Sebastian stopped by Marley's room with his armor in tow. "Marley, why are you still in bed? Let's go. Grab your things and come on. Hurry up!"

"I don't know where my armor is! I don't know where anything is! I don't even know where I am!" Marley shouted.

"Okay, so you are still with this madness, eh?" David Sebastian put his armor down, grabbed Marley's armor from his wardrobe, placed it in a rucksack, and handed it to him. "Follow me, little brother! We are going to be late. Oh, and we're stopping by the nurse's station after today's lesson. Apparently, you hit your head or something."

"Lesson?" Marley asked. "Is Judah coming?"

"No, he will stay here with his caretakers until our morning lesson is done just as he does every day. Now stop asking so many questions and let's go."

David Sebastian grabbed his bag. Marley grabbed his and

followed David Sebastian .

As they trekked through the halls of the enormous castle, Marley looked around in amazement . The castle's ceilings were as high as the sky. There was marble and gold all around. He could see rooms everywhere that he turned his head. The halls were lined with the kind of fancy pillars and statues that Marley had only before seen on his school field trips to the museum.

As the boys continued to walk the long halls, Marley looked to his left where he saw the most amazing view he had ever seen. The castle sat on top of a mountain. Marley was now in the big blue sky that he had always admired as a little boy. He could see birds flying and playing in the air, and it amazed him. The boys continued to walk through the huge castle until they finally arrived at the chow hall.

"Marley, hand your armor to Daniel," David Sebastian said as he did the same and walked into the chow hall.

Marley did so and followed his big brother to the chow line. Marley motioned to grab a plate.

"Little brother, come here," David Sebastian whispered to Marley to not embarrass him in front of their trainees. "What are you doing? You know that we eat after the others eat. We are princes, and we make sure our cadets are well fed before we eat. Come on. Let's go see how everyone is doing."

Marley and David Sebastian went to meet with the other boys. After all of the trainees had gotten their plates, the two young princes got in line for their food. After they'd gotten their food, they sat with the others at one of the many huge tables in the hall and began to eat.

"Time's up!" Daniel shouted shortly after the boys began to eat. "Everyone put your plates away and head to the War

Room!"

Marley got up from the table, swallowing his last bit of food.

"War Room?" he asked while following David Sebastian to put their plates away. "I haven't even finished eating. That wasn't enough time."

"Little brother..." David Sebastian said as he looked at Marley and shook his head.

Then the boys all marched down to the War Room to attend their daily lesson.

8

Chapter 8: Lost at 13

Marley followed David Sebastian to the front of the classroom where they both took a seat. The other boys were already seated and talking among themselves.

Daniel, the man from the chow hall, was at the back of the classroom standing at the door. He occasionally cracked the door and looked out as if he were looking for something or someone. Daniel suddenly shouted, "Group! Attention!"

The boys all stopped what they were doing and stood up with their arms to their sides. Their hands were in fists, and their heads and eyes were straight forward.

Marley hesitated to stand; but as always, his big brother was there to correct him.

David Sebastian grabbed Marley by the arm, made him stand, and said, "Do as I do."

In walked a tall dark man with long curly gray hair in a slicked back ponytail wearing glasses.

The man walked to the front of the huge classroom and said with a commanding voice, "Take a seat!"

The boys all sat.

"Another of our cadets has disappeared," Professor Addiex notified his class. "If you haven't noticed, which each of you should have because you *are* your brother's keeper, there is an empty seat in class today. Cadet Stellan is missing. Yesterday was his thirteenth birthday. We've received notification from his parents that when they went to his chamber this morning when he didn't show for breakfast, he was not there. We can officially say now that there is a pattern here. Boys are disappearing on their thirteenth birthdays without a trace. The boys tend to disappear from in or around their homes. There have been no reports of forced entry. There also have been no sightings of unidentified individuals near the village or near the castle. We have a group of soldiers out looking for him. There will be no class today. Be vigilant and do not leave the court's premises. Class is dismissed. Prince David Sebastian and Prince Marley, report at once to the Throne Room. Your father, the king, is awaiting your presence.""Yes, sir," David Sebastian said.

Professor Addiex looked at Marley as he didn't reply.

"Yes, sir," said Marley.

9

Chapter 9: My Father, the King

Marley and David Sebastian left the classroom. As they entered the hallway, a concerned Marley asked, "David, you do realize that my thirteenth birthday is tomorrow? Don't you?""I know, little brother, now let's go. Father is waiting on us, and the king waits for no one for too long."

The boys hurried down the hall to meet their father, King Leigh.

The boys entered the Throne Room and walked the long red carpet to their father's throne. David Sebastian bowed before his father, and Marley followed suit.

"Father, you summoned us?" David Sebastian asked as the boys rose before the king.

King Leigh stood before his sons. King Leigh was a tall man, and he looked very strong, as he was. He wore a crown on top of his long wavy salt- and- pepper hair. The king stepped down from his throne to get closer to his sons. Then, surprisingly to Marley, he greeted them both with a hug.

"Sons, I'm certain that you are aware of the disappearances of your fellow brothers in arms. As you may also know, a pattern has been established for those who have gone missing. They are all boys who disappear on their thirteenth birthday. This is the crucial age, as you know, when a boy becomes a man in our kingdom and in others. I believe that whoever is responsible for these disappearances has an overall plan that goes far beyond what meets the eye. This said, Marley, with tomorrow being your thirteenth birthday, you are not to leave your chamber until further notice. The guards to your right will follow you to your room and remain there until it is safe for you to come out. Understood?"

Marley looked frightened, but he simply bowed his head and replied, "Yes, Father."

King Leigh then looked at Marley's brother. "David Sebastian make sure you are at knight training in the morning."

"Yes, Father," said David Sebastian.

"You are both dismissed."

The boys bowed as their father returned to his throne. They left the Throne Room and walked down the hall to their rooms closely followed by the guards that their father had assigned to watch Marley.

10

Chapter 10: Innocent Deception

Marley's guards opened and closed his chamber doors for him. He heard the doors lock behind him.

One of the guards called out, "At ease."

Marley looked through his peephole to see if the guards stood outside of his door, and just as King Leigh had told the princes they would be, they were. Marley let out a big sigh.

He turned from the doors to see Judah standing inches before him! He was startled and jumped a little!

"Judah! You scared me."

Judah looked confused.

Marley petted Judah on his head and said, "It's okay, buddy."

Judah purred, walked over to Marley's bed, and lay down next to it.

Marley was exhausted and still confused. *How did I get here?* he wondered. *Why does everyone know me, yet I seem to know no one?*

He plopped on the bed fully clothed, with his shoes hanging from the edge . Marley knew better than to have his shoes on any bed in this realm or any other. He closed his eyes and fell asleep. Hours into his slumber, Marley heard a loud noise that woke him. He heard a boy crying outside. The boy's voice seemed to get closer with each passing second. Marley looked outside and saw a young boy carrying a torch screaming, "Help me! Someone help me please!"

Marley looked behind the boy to see what had him so frightened. He saw nothing. The boy continued to run and scream. Now Marley could see a figure chasing him.

"Judah!" Marley called out. "I need you to take me down there to help him."

Judah knelt down beside Marley. Marley mounted Judah, and just like that, Judah spread his wings and flew down several stories below to the ground. Marley saw the young boy running at a distance.

"Follow him, Judah!" Marley exclaimed.

Judah ran behind the boy. As he got a few feet away from him, the boy ran behind a tree. Marley and Judah followed, but to their surprise, they no longer saw the boy. Emerging from behind the tree, in his place, was someone else.

11

Chapter 11: The Meeting

"Hello, Marley. I've been dying to meet you for some time, young man," said a man who was leaning against the tree that Marley saw the boy run behind. The dapper man wore a black top hat, a black tailored suit, and a black shirt and tie. He snickered, gave a quick grimace, and said, "Happy thirteenth birthday, sir."

"Tomorrow is my birthday. And who are you? What happened to the boy that ran through here crying? Did you not see him? Did you not hear him? Did you not see a black lion chasing him?" Marley asked, panicked, confused, and out of breath.

"Oh, but, Marley, it is midnight, young man. Trust me, I know when your birthday is. I've waited for the very day, the very hour, the minute, the second to see this very day! I've waited years for this exact moment in time. More years than your mind could even conceive."

Marley stared at the man.

"You see, you are very special young lad. The universe has waited for your arrival. You have been called the chosen one, the peace bringer, the overcomer. Some have even referred to you as the savior." He laughed. "Can you believe that, Marley? You, the savior? Just what and who is it that you think you can save, Marley? Please do tell me. As I stand here eagerly before you, all I see is a puny little boy, not a man. What is it that you think you can stop or begin?"

"I believe you have me confused with someone else. How do you know who I am? Right now, I don't know where I am, let alone why I'm here or exactly how it is that I got here. I'm beginning to question who I am altogether. I don't belong here. This isn't my home, so I'm fairly certain that there has been some sort of mix- up. In fact, I believe this all must be a dream or some sort of delusion."

"Oh, you belong here, Marley, and this is all so very real. It has always been your destiny to be in this very spot at this very moment. Just because right now you don't know who you are, the powers you possess, and all that you're capable of, it doesn't make you any less of a threat to me. You see, I have been told that you will someday be my undoing. I don't know when that day might be. It might be years down the line, or it might be tomorrow. Either way, you see—" He moved closer to Marley. "I can't. Ever. Allow. That. Day. To. Come!"

He took off his hat and waved it in a circle, creating a large wind gust. A portal opened. Marley stood there for a moment gazing at the portal in shock and terror before he turned and tried to run.

The man let out a quick chuckle. "Now where do you think you're going?" He turned his wrist, and with his palm facing upward and finger pointing toward Marley, he drew him into the portal without laying a finger on him. Marley screamed as they traveled through the portal. It was a quick trip, but to Marley it seemed like forever. Marley landed with a thud, facedown on the ground, while his captor landed smoothly on his feet as though he had already done this before.

"Welcome to your own personal nightmare, Prince," he said as he brushed his suit sleeves off and put his hat back on. "It's not where you've been, or where you think you are, but it is where you shall be for eternity. If that makes sense to you." He laughed a wicked laugh. "That is unless you can manage to escape. I should let you know in advance that you won't be able to accomplish that feat. No one ever has. You think you're special, but you see, you're not. There are three roads that you can take from here. The road to the left, the one to the right, or the road straight ahead. Only one road will lead you out of here. I have the feeling you shall remain trapped for all time, so get comfy. Enjoy." The man once again took his hat off and waved it, opening the portal that they came through.

He turned to walk into the portal when Marley asked, "Are you really going to leave me here?"

The man continued to walk toward the portal not acknowledging Marley's question.

Marley cried, "No! Wait! Please don't leave me here! I've done nothing to deserve this!"The man turned to Marley and said, "You're right, Marley. You've done nothing to deserve this, but as you may have been told before, life isn't fair. You're here because of who you are, not because of what you have done. You're not just any boy who just turned thirteen. You're *the* boy who just turned thirteen . So, you, sir, will get an extra special touch of cruelty on your journey. Oh, and stop crying, will you? It's, uh, what's the word that I'm looking for?" He paused to think. "Oh yeah, pathetic. Toodaloo."

"At least tell me your name. What is your name?" Marley

yelled.

"Lord Lefleur the Third, to be exact, if you must know. But you'll simply remember me as your ending." He smiled, adjusted his tie, turned back around, a nd walked into the portal.

The portal closed, and Marley was left alone in the middle of nowhere surrounded by rows of large oak trees covered with moss. He stood in front of the three dirt roads with a life-threatening decision to make.

12

Chapter 12: Where Is Marley?

Judah flew back to the castle and into Marley's room and began to scratch at the door, letting out a thunderous roar. The guards opened the door to check on the prince.

"What's wrong, Judah?" asked one of the guards.

Judah ran to Marley's bed and continued to roar. The guards followed him.

"Where is Prince Marley?" one of the guards shouted.

"The king will not be pleased with us," another guard said to himself as he put his hands on his fore head.Then the guards ran down the halls to the king's chamber.

"We wish to speak with King Leigh," they said, almost out of breath from running.

"The king is not here." One of King Leigh's personal door guards answered.

The guards turned immediately and once again ran down the halls. They knew that there was only one other place that King Leigh would be at this time of night—the War Room.

They ran there and saluted the guards at the door. One of them said, "We have grave news for King Leigh. I need to talk to him right now."

The War Room guard returned his salute and moved aside for the guards to enter.

King Leigh was at his desk, looking at a map in front of him. He had his hand on his head and was in deep thought.

The guards knelt before the king.

"Your Majesty, permission to speak freely."

"At ease. Permission granted," he said in a solemn voice as he looked down at the map on his desk.

The guards stood. One said to the king as his voice slightly trembled and sweat beads rolled down his face, "Your Highness, Marley is not in his room." He paused and hung his head before saying, "He is gone."

King Leigh looked up from the map on his desk and said, "Excuse me. I don't think I heard you quite right. Say it again."

"Your Majesty, we stood outside the doors of Marley's chambers as you instructed, never leaving. We don't know what happened or how it happened, but Marley is not there."

King Leigh, being the even- tempered and strong king that he was, calmly said to the guard, "Call a formation at once in the courtyard. You have fifteen minutes before I will stand before you."

"Yes, Your Majesty." The guards bowed, turned, and ran from the room in a hurry to gather the soldiers for formation.

T welve minutes later, all the kingdom's soldiers were gathered in its courtyard in a perfect formation as King Leigh had requested. The courtyard was magnificent. It was perfectly bricked and landscaped. There were many different types of flowers, shrubbery, and trees. The most noticeable of trees were the cherry blossoms, a special touch of the queen.

Exactly fifteen minutes later, a trumpet sounded as King

Leigh appeared at the front of the formation.

The commander of the formation called in a loud and thunderous voice, "Kingdom, *attention*!"

The formation came to attention. The commander turned to King Leigh. King Leigh called to the formation with a loud and powerful voice, "At ease."

The formation moved to rest.

King Leigh continued, "As you all know, Prince Marley has disappeared. He was last seen in his room last night. There were guards outside of his door, and so the only way he could have gotten out is if Judah flew him down or if someone somehow went up to his room and took him. After this formation, you all are to disperse at once and do all that you can to find him."

The king came to attention and said, "Kingdom, attention! Fall out."

The soldiers dispersed and began a vigorous hunt for Prince Marley.

13

Chapter 13: Chosen Path, Again

After standing there for what felt like an eternity , Marley chose to go down the road that was straight ahead for no reason other than the fact that it could be a way for him to get home. There was nothing surrounding him but trees. As Marley walked for some time, he found himself back where he started. But the strange thing was that Marley hadn't walked in a circle to get back to the beginning. Marley was confused, but he kept on. He then tried the road to the left and found himself back where he had started . Then he tried the road to the right. Again, back to the beginning. Marley tried each path again with the same result. He now realized that Lord Lefleur never meant for him to escape. He would be trapped in this new warped reality for an eternity.

The sun was setting, and Marley became more afraid as darkness quickly overtook the sky. He smirked and said to himself, "I'm dreaming. Yes, that's it. I never woke up. I'm dreaming. Am I crazy to believe that I am actually a prince in a faraway land?"

He laughed. He began to think of ways to wake himself. He

pinched himself. That didn't work. He pulled his hair. Nothing. He slapped himself in the face! Still there. Marley was desperate to awaken! He turned to his left as he remembered passing a small body of water. He ran over, knelt, cupped both of his hands, and took some water from the lake. He closed his eyes and splashed the water on his face. Marley paused for a moment, wiped the water from his eyes, and then slowly opened them. He realized, with water dripping from his face, that nothing had changed. He began to softly cry.

"Mom," he said as he cried. "Mom." His calls grew louder. "*Mom!* Wake me up! Granny! Help me! I'm stuck here! I need you! Please! Wake me up!"

Marley continued to cry. He felt defeated. He was so tired that he lay next to the water in the grass. Suddenly, a bright light flashed across the sky. Marley's pendant that his grandfather had given him caught the reflection of the light, drawing Marley's attention to it. Now, Marley could clearly see the details of the pendant. He grabbed the lion's head pendant and said, "Judah," before he closed his eyes and fell asleep.

14

Chapter 14: Split Decision

"Aaaaggghhh!" Marley awakened, frightened from his sleep and screaming. "Judah?" he said, breathing quickly. "What are you doing here?"

"Sir, you called me, and so I came right away. You were asleep when I got here, and so I let you get some rest. I can imagine that after all you've been through, it is much needed," Judah said.

"Wawawawa . . . waitttttttt one minute! Are you talking tooo meee right now? No one said that you can talk!"

"No one knows that I can talk. You are the only one who can understand what I'm saying, sir."

"Why are you calling me 'sir'? Do flying lions call people 'sir'? And I'm just a boy. I'm not a 'sir.'"

"I call you 'sir' as a sign of respect, and you are more than just a boy, sir. You will see someday soon."

"So why didn't you talk to me before?"

"There was no need to speak at the moment, sir. This is somewhat of an especially perplexing situation you have yourself in. Let's go."

Marley replied, "I'm pretty sure it's not that simple to just fly out of here."

"Sir, how do you think I got in? We will leave the same way."

Marley climbed onto Judah's back, and in the blink of an eye, they took off into the big bright blue sky. It wasn't long after that Marley and Judah could see the portal that Judah had entered to rescue Marley. Judah began to fly more quickly as they approached the portal. At that moment, Marley noticed a makeshift tent city below them.

"Judah! Do you see that?"

"Yes, I see it, sir."

"Is anyone living there?" Marley asked Judah.

"I'm not sure if there is anyone living there at the moment, sir. But at the very least, there once was."

"We have to go down to see if there is anyone there who may need our help."

"Sir, we only have so much time to make it into this portal. It will soon close. We need to leave now while we can."

"Judah, we can't just leave. If there are people down there, they are probably stuck here like I was. We can fly them out of here back to wherever it is that they are from."

"Sir, only you and I can enter this portal. It won't allow anyone else to pass through."

"Why is that? That can't be the case! Are you sure?" Marley continued to yell as the sound of the wind was overtaking their conversation.

"I am sure, sir! You and I are the only ones who can pass through the portal! So, you have a decision to make, and you don't have much time to make it! Do you want to go home, or do you want to go down to see if there are others here who need our help? There is no guarantee that we will make it back home if we don't enter this portal right now."

"Judah, I don't know what to do! I mean, if there are people down there, will I be able to help them? I'm just a boy! It was different when I thought we could just fly them home, but I don't know if I'll be able to find us another way out!"

Judah and Marley were seconds away from entering the portal when Judah firmly shouted, "Prince Marley, sir, you need to decide! Now!"

The prince decided. "Let's see if there are others! Fly down!"

"If there is anyone there, certainly we have been seen already so there is no sense in trying to conceal ourselves. Do you see the largest tent there, Marley?"

"Yes, Judah, I see it."

"I will land there beside it. It looks as though it may be or may have been some sort of headquarters for the camp. If we're going to get answers from anywhere, more than likely it will be from there."

At once, Judah began to descend. The portal in the sky quickly closed with no trace of it ever being present. The terrible thing was, though, the portal didn't close before what Judah thought was the impossible occurred. A spirit as dark as night and as ghastly as anyone's most frightening nightmare slipped into the portal from this desolate land and entered King Leigh's home, the Kingdom of Savagna.

15

Chapter 15: Dark Shadows

The search for Marley in the vast kingdom was far and wide. All the kingdom's soldiers, to include Prince David Sebastation, searched for Prince Marley . Suddenly, huge gusts of winds swept the land. The trees violently swayed, and a furious dust storm began. The soldiers worked hard to walk against the wind and stinging grains of dust. Many of their helmets flew away.

Then, as suddenly as the wind began, it ended, and the soldiers stopped in their tracks . Then there was thunder and lightning, but no rain. A terrifying loud moaning noise echoed throughout the sky. The dark thing that had made it through to the other side of the portal revealed itself to the land. It had no form. It had no face. It resembled a black cloud, but it was clear that this was no cloud. There was something far more sinister about this evilness. It floated high above the trees and briefly hovered in one spot. Then a pitch-black darkness fell over the kingdom as though it were night, but it was still hours away from sunset. The cloud began moving again, traveling in the direction of King Leigh's castle, leaving behind a trail of darkness in its path.

16

Chapter 16: They're Here

As Judah said he would, he landed on the side of the large tent. Marley climbed off Judah and looked around.

The silence was deafening. The ground was dry and without grass. No one was in sight, but the camp had clearly recently been lived in as shown by half- eaten dishes of food left lying around and smoke coming from a stack of logs as though a fire had just been burning there.

Judah knelt so that Marley could dismount him. Marley quietly did so. Judah motioned his head toward the front of the tent, and they both began to walk in that direction. Once at the tent's front, they saw its entrance.

Judah said in as low of a voice as he could and speaking as briefly and as concisely as he could, "Sir, it's very important that you follow my instructions. Stay behind me and against this wall. On my count of three, we enter. Go in and immediately turn to your right moving along the wall. If we encounter any dangers, I will do my best to protect us both, but you must always be brave and attempt to protect yourself from here on out. Understood, sir?"

Marley nodded .

"Sir, I need for you to verbally acknowledge that you understand me."

"Yes, Judah, I understand."

Judah counted, "One, two, three."

The two quickly moved into the tent.

Once inside, Judah and Marley saw that there was no one in the tent. Marley began to breathe deeply as he was relieved that there were no threats in sight. He noticed a stench in the air and hurried to cover his nose so he would no longer smell the foul aroma. They walked farther inside along the wall, when the two noticed multiple makeshift mats on the ground that were made of thin and tattered pieces of cloth on top of hay. The indentations in the mats indicated that people had recently slept on them.

"It's obvious that not long ago people were here. Where on earth could they have possibly gone so quickly?" asked Marley.

"I don't know, sir. That's—"

The two heard a crashing sound. A chest had tipped over in the middle of the tent. They began to walk toward it to examine its contents. The chest had all the items you would see in a treasure chest; but most noticeable was a large sum of gold coins that had spilled all over the ground.

"Judah, can you tell me exactly how in the world this managed to fall over on its own?"

Then the coins on the ground began to move. Judah and Marley looked closely to see that the coins were moving to form the shape of shoeprints! The prints quickly multiplied! The prints were now out of the coins, onto the dirt, and heading toward the tent's entrance!

"Stop! Who's there?" Marley shouted. The footprints

continued. "I said stop!"

Judah flapped his wings just enough to get off the ground and flew to block the tent's entrance. The prints stopped in their tracks.

"Reveal yourself!" Judah said, but nothing happened. "Now!" he roared.

A young, tall, and slender man with long locks and dark skin slowly appeared before Judah as he removed a head wrap. He stared at Judah and didn't seem to be frightened of him.

"Who are you, why are you hiding, and why are you trying to escape instead of helping us? I know you heard our conversation," Judah asked the handsome young man.

"I'm Pierre Lauren, and I don't insert myself into business that does not pertain to me. I was merely trying to get out of here without further involving myself in this madness that I've found myself in. Now if you have no further line of questioning for me, I'll be leaving now."

Pierre began to walk toward the entrance.

"You aren't going anywhere, young lad. I suggest you have a seat or lie down on one of those piles of hay over there," Judah said in a calm yet firm tone as he lightly placed his paw on Pierre and slightly moved him back.

Pierre did as Judah commanded.

Judah then said to Pierre as Marley looked through the contents of the fallen chest, "Tell me where you're from, everything you know about this place, and everything you've seen and heard since you've been here."

"I am the prince of Atlantus, your neighboring kingdom."

Marley looked up from the chest holding a golden book and said with a puzzled look on his face, "How do you know you live in a kingdom neighboring ours?"

"Marley, your father is a very powerful and well-known ruler, and therefore, his family is also well known. Everyone knows who you are, Prince Marley." Pierre slightly bowed his head in respect when he said Marley's name. "Now would you like for me to continue answering your pet's questions, or is there something else that you would like to know?"

Marley shook his head at Pierre and redirected his attention to the book that he was holding.

"It was nightfall in my kingdom. I was in the courtyard preparing to go inside when I heard a voice cry out for help." Marley again turned his attention to Pierre. "That voice sounded very much like my brother Phillip who had been missing for over a year, and so I followed it. As I came upon what looked like him, a sharp man in a suit appeared in front of me, and now I'm here. I suppose you had a similar fate."

Marley nodded in agreement. Judah looked on intensely.

Pierre continued, "Not long after I arrived here, I was discovered by one of the keepers of the boys. I had fallen asleep against a tree after tiring myself out trying to make it back home. And might I say what a pleasant rest it was when I was found before I could put my head wrap on to conceal myself."

"How does that work? Your head wrap I mean? Are you supposed to possess magic or something?" Marley asked.

"My family has a certain set of powers. If magic is what you'd like to call it, then whatever floats your boat. Is it so far-fetched for me to have powers, Prince Marley, when you are walking around here with a talking pet lion that can fly? Do tell."

Marley got up and walked toward Pierre. "You know what? I'm growing a little impatient with your mouth," he said to Pierre.

"Sir! As you were!" said Judah firmly.

Savagna's prince returned to his former position and again shook his head at Pierre.

Pierre continued, "I suppose I'll be able to finish this story uninterrupted at some point today. Now I've lost my train of thought. What was I even saying? Oh yeah, and so I was brought here to this camp, to this tent that was filled with many other boys that appeared to be famished and fatigued. We were fed scraps of bread and given sips of water. They apparently wanted to give us just enough to keep us alive to carry out whatever mission they clearly had planned for us. They were preparing to move us to another location when I snuck away from my sleeping place, hid in a corner, and donned my head wrap. They looked for me, but I was hiding in plain sight. They couldn't find me, and so they left without me."

Judah asked, "Did they mention where they were going?"

"They didn't, but after the last person exited the tent, I ran from my corner to see which direction they were traveling. They kept a straight path from the tent's entrance into the woods."From above, the three of them heard a noise so loud that it sounded as though the sky opened; and in fact, it had!

"We must go and in a hurry! That's the exact sound I heard each time someone new arrived here!" Pierre said firmly.

"They're likely preparing to bring in another group of boys," Prince Marley said.

"Great observation, but we really don't have time for this. I meant now!" Pierre exclaimed. "And you," Pierre said, pointing at Judah, "*do not fly* or you will expose us. Follow me!"

They hurriedly exited the tent and ran into the dark and cold woods. The trees were bare, showing their naked branches. Strange sounds of animal life echoed about, but there were none to be seen. Marley was nervous, as would be any young lad. He turned his head nearly every second in fear that danger was closely lurking in the shadows.

"Do you hear that?" a strange voice yelled out from the distance. "Someone's there! Look, there they are! After them!" the voice continued.

Judah crouched. "Hop on! Now!" he roared.

Once the princes were on, Judah ran so fast that he could've taken off in flight, but he didn't so that they would not draw any more attention to themselves than they already had. Judah dipped and dodged between the trees. The sound of withered and dried leaves rustled beneath his paws, and fallen twigs snapped with each step as they fled.

Judah ran over hills covered in damp, almost dead grass and crossed muddy streams of water. The splashes of water although dirty were refreshing for just a second, but there was no time to revel in that comfort.

Judah continued to run, then he approached a lone bush with nothing in its circumference for a mile. It had a bright light beside it. Judah came to an abrupt halt. He turned away from the light, and they all looked from where they came to see that their pursuers were getting closer by the second.

"Sirs, what do you want to do? The choice is yours to make."

In that instant, Marley thought of his mother's and granny's sweet faces. After all that had recently happened to him, he didn't know who his actual family was. Regardless, he knew that he had to do anything in his power to try to make it back to them, in case they were his actual family and not just a part of a dream.

"Go into the light, Judah!" a confused Prince Marley shouted.

"At once, sir. Hold on tight, princes!" Judah replied.

Then he ran full speed into the light.

17

Chapter 17: The Dark Castle

The three entered yet another dimension. Judah landed on his feet, and with the boys still on his back, he turned around to see if anyone had followed them into the light. No one had. The portal had already closed.

Judah turned back around. "Are you two all right?" he calmly asked the princes as he knelt so they could dismount him. Judah shook and stretched his wings.

"Yes," they both answered in unison.

"Judah…" Marley said as he swallowed hard and pointed north. "Look."

Judah and Pierre directed their focus to where Marley pointed. In the distance was an enormous castle standing tall and strong and composed of an endless number of towers. It was black with gold trim and one of the most beautiful sights Marley had ever seen. The sky surrounding the castle was gray, but clear. The grass and flowers were shades of navy blue, deep violet, and gray. The trees had burnt- orange leaves and turquoise trunks and were draped with beautiful gray moss. It was an unbelievably gorgeous sight.

"Let's go," Marley said. "The boys must be in there."

"I'm fairly certain they are, young prince," Judah said. "But we must be careful in approaching the castle. Trust me. It won't be so easy as to just waltz in the castle and set the boys free."

Marley looked at Judah, then at the castle, then back to Judah with a little smirk.

After a brief pause, Marley took off in a sprint, running toward the castle. Pierre and Judah followed. They ran up a hill, down a hill, and up again! They stumbled over rocks and tree roots, got tangled in hanging vines, and tripped over rough patches of grass. They ran down one final hill before coming to a sudden stop. Rocks fell from beneath their feet to the water down below. They had come upon a cliff that separated them from the gargantuan castle.

"What is this? Are you kidding me?" Marley asked. "Judah, can you fly us over?"

"I can't, Prince Marley. They may not know that we are here. We would be too obvious if I flew us over, and this time, we are too close to rescuing the others for us to risk exposing ourselves any more than is necessary. Let's try to rest and figure out a more discreet way to make it over."

The three sat in the colorful grass, all breathing heavily from their adventurous dash.

"What's that?" Pierre asked. "Did you all hear that?"

"Yes, I did. Take cover, princes," Judah said just loud enough to be heard by the young men.

They all concealed themselves behind trees.

"There's no reason to be afraid," called out a gentle, strong voice. "I am here for the same reason as you. I saw you when you entered through the portal. You may reveal yourselves."

"How do we know we can trust you? Why didn't you say

anything to us when you first saw us?" Marley called out from his hiding spot.

"I wanted to know your intentions before I said anything to you. My brother Duke is in that castle. I've been trapped in this realm trying to rescue him. I know a way to the castle, but it's what happens once you're there that I am unable to face alone. But now that I have help..."

Marley, Judah, and Pierre all revealed themselves to the stranger one by one.The three were stunned by what they saw when they came from their hiding places.

"What —what —what is your name?" Marley stuttered.

"Nakkiran. Princess of Champus."

Nakirran was gorgeously breathtaking. Her skin was dark and smooth, and her hair was a beautiful full mane, long, black, thick, and curly. Her eyes were almond- shaped and a shade of brown so dark it seemed to hide her innermost thoughts, fears, secrets, and pain. Her lips were as full as her figure. She stood strong. You could tell by the way she carried herself that she, too, was a warrior. Nakirran wore a colorful hooded cape over her clothing.

"My name is—" Prince Marley started.

"There is no need for the formal introduction," Nakirran said, interrupting Prince Marley. "I know who you are, Prince Marley. I've heard of you from the time that I was a little girl. The description that I've been given of you throughout the years matches your appearance to the letter, right down to your piercing hazel eyes."

Marley blushed.

"Ahem, I'm sorry to interrupt, but, Nakirran, how do we get to the castle?" Prince Pierre asked.

"There is a chant that I've heard several say upon approaching the castle. The chant causes a drawbridge to lower so that we can cross. It took me a few tries to perfect the chant, but I was finally able to lower the bridge. But I never crossed it."

"So, what happens when the bridge is lowered?" Marley gathered his thoughts just enough to be able to talk to the beautiful princess.

"There is battle," Nakirran calmly yet assertively responded . "Other worldly soldiers appear once the bridge is lowered to protect the castle. I've only seen one battle take place when two thieves tried to enter the palace to steal jewels. Apparently, they had been watching the palace for quite some time as I have in order to learn how to lower the bridge. Finally, after quite a few attempts, they lowered the bridge, even made it across it, but they shortly thereafter encountered the inhuman soldiers. Let's just say they never made it into the castle to see any jewels, and they never again crossed the bridge. There is not much on which I can brief you. The battle was short, and the thieves were gone without ever being physically touched. Just be prepared for someone, or should I say something, to come at you at any moment and from any angle." Nakirran stopped and then asked Marley, "Are you prepared for such an undertaking, Prince Marley?"

Marley looked at Prince Pierre and then Judah before he firmly replied to conceal his fear, "I am, Princess Nakirran."

"Judah, Pierre," Marley continued. "How about you? Are you prepared for battle?"

"Do I have any other choice? No? Then yes," Pierre responded.

"Yes, sir, but first I need to have a quick word with you," Judah said.

18

Chapter 18: The Inheritance

Judah turned and walked a few feet away to speak with the prince in confidence.

"What is it, Judah?" Marley asked.

"Prince, you need to know that there are special abilities that you possess—"

Marley interrupted Judah . "Special abilities? What kind of special abilities?" he asked.

"You inherited a special trait that gives you powers, if you will. However, like your other family members, your powers were not able to be manifested until your thirteenth birthday. Most of what you learn about your powers, you will discover at the very moment you need them. The ability to win comes from within, young sir. Now, you possess all that you need to accomplish what you've decided to accomplish. Your abilities will strengthen with time. Never doubt yourself and always speak and walk with great confidence."

Marley looked puzzled. "And after all that we've been through, why are you just telling me this now, my dear friend?" he asked.

"I wanted to wait for the right time, and that time is now, sir.

Let's advance."

"Forward march," called King Leigh's son.

A nd they all moved forward, until they came to a halt at the cliff's edge.

19

Chapter 19: The Bridge

Nakirran stepped forward without fear. She stretched her hands toward the castle and calmly but strongly chanted, "The boys they cross, one by one, they cross the boys. *Eht masc yeht cruzar singulatim, yeht cruz eht masc.*"

There was a brief moment of silence followed by a cool breeze. Nakirran's beautiful black hair blew in the wind. The atmosphere in the strange land was changing. Dark gray clouds began to surround the castle. The sound of thunder startled the quad, there was lightning in the distance, and a cold rain began to fall.

Baffled, Nakirran looked back at the others and said, "This is unusual." She then turned back to face the castle. At that moment, she saw the bridge she had mentioned slowly appearing from the point where she stood over to the castle's edge. It was a black stone bridge with gold beams and accents that matched the castle. When it was fully formed, a figure appeared at its end closest to the castle. They saw that the figure was a soldier wearing a suit of black, silver, and golden armor. He held a sword with a golden hilt and a blade of a shiny black steel. One by one, more soldiers began to appear. There were thirteen in total.

Marley moved in front of the princess.

20

Chapter 20: Becoming

"Who are you?" Marley called out to the soldiers.

One soldier laughed. "You dare speak to me? Why don't you come a little closer and find out, prince?"

"How do you know I'm a prince?" Marley replied as he wiped rain from his face.

"We are the Alzheiran soldiers, and we've been serving this palace's king for centuries. There is a lot that we know. Besides, we were told to eventually expect your company. Come on over."

"How do we know we can trust you?" Marley asked.

"Who said that you can trust me, boy?" the Alzheir yelled with a menacing grimace. "You don't want to come over?" He laughed. "Then we'll come to you. *Dūblé marcs!*" the soldier cried out. Then he and his men began to hurriedly advance across the bridge.

Marley turned his head and shouted, "Judah!"

Judah called back, "Prince! Remember what I told you! It is time!"

Marley turned his head back, took a deep breath, and then uttered in a low voice, "You all stay behind."

"But, sir," Judah protested. "I did not mean for you to do this alone."

"I said stay behind!" Marley ran full speed toward the Alzheir. About one quarter of the way across the bridge, something unexpected occurred. The soldiers' feet left the bridge, and they were flying without wings toward Marley and the others.

"You won't remember any of this or anything else when I'm done with you. You will serve our king one way or another, disobedient brat. The one true king!"

Marley suddenly stopped. He looked down and saw that his pendant was glowing! He grabbed the pendant and aimed it toward the soldiers. Just as Marley did this, the soldier put his sword in the air and lunged it toward Marley.

Then Marley powerfully shouted, *"Cadere et gravi somno sopitos!"*

There was a flash of bright light. The soldiers all dropped and fell into a deep sleep.

Marley stood there for a moment, quiet in amazement at what he had done. He held on to the pendant and looked at it in shock as raindrops fell from his face and his locks.

Then he quickly snapped to and checked the soldiers to see if it was okay to pass. When he saw that it was, he called back for the others. The group was able to cross the bridge with ease, thanks to the brave prince. Their hardest obstacle was stepping over their fallen enemies on the way across. Once they had made it , the bridge again disappeared into the dark.

"Let me get ahead," Nakirran called as she began to quickly walk from the rear.

"No. Stay where you are. It's too dangerous. I'll be the first to go in," Marley replied.

Nakirran continued to walk forward until she was in front of the group. She turned and grabbed Marley's hand and said, "Trust me."

Marley nervously swallowed and replied, "I trust you, Princess Nakirran."

Nakirran turned back. Once at the door, the princess placed her hand on it. A white light appeared outlining her hand. She pressed forward and walked through the door into the castle.

21

Chapter 21: Miserable Bliss

Nakirran opened the door for the others.

"What was that?" Marley asked.

"If I can physically touch it, I can go through it; but we have no time to further discuss it at the moment. Come inside."

The group entered the massive castle and began to walk through its main hall in two line s, one on each side of the hall. Portraits of soldiers that looked like those that the group had just encountered hang on the walls.

Pierre suddenly turned his head and looked behind him. "Is it just me or does it seem that their eyes are following us?" he quietly asked of the portraits' subjects.

"I think we're all just tired, Pierre, but we must remain focused. We can be attacked at any moment. Keep your heads on the swivel and walk swiftly," Prince Marley said.

They quickly advanced through the halls, alert for signs of any threat. Marley and Judah were on one side. Nakirran and Pierre were on the other. They walked so quickly through the halls that they didn't have time to observe much about the castle's odd beauty other than the sets of shiny knights' armor that boldly stood along the walls. It wasn't long before they came upon a pair of golden double doors adorned with rubies and emeralds.

"Do you hear that? No, it couldn't be. It sounds as though the boys may be in there; but that would be entirely too easy," Marley said, questioning the ease of it all.

Pierre said, "Look, if you think I'm going in there, you are *sadly* mistaken. If the boys *are* in there, this is clearly a setup."

Marley replied, "We have no choice but to go in. Some of us are here by choice, while others are not; but one way or the other, we're not leaving this palace without rescuing the boys. On my count of three, we go in. I'll be the first to enter, Judah, you next, then Pierre, and lastly the princess. Princess Nakirran, stay near the door. If anything happens to us, you run and don't look back."

"I don't need any special treatment because I'm a girl, Marley," Nakirran firmly said.

"I believe that with every ounce of me, but that doesn't mean that I still won't do my best to protect you. Now on the count of three . . . one, two, three."

Marley turned the large handles on the doors and entered the room, then Judah, Pierre, and Nakirran entered.

Behind the massive doors, in the great room, were a number of boys that looked as though they were close to Marley's age. Some dined and played games at the table in the center of the room; others played music, danced, and watched the jesters entertain them while laughing the heartiest laughs that anyone could imagine hearing. Marley spotted his missing classmate Stellan aiming a bow and arrow at a target. He seemed to be having the best time of his life. It was at this moment Marley realized without a doubt in his mind that the missing boys had been found. Pierre saw his brother Phillip dancing, and Nakirran's brother Duke indulged on fine cheeses and fruits at the main table.

"Room! Attention!" called one of the boys before any of them had a moment to address their friend or brother.

The boys stood. Time seemed to stand still. The music, laughter, and entertainment all came to a halt. In walked Lord Lefleur. "Prince Marley, you finally made it. Welcome, young man."

"What is this place and what do you want with all of these boys?" asked Marley.

Lord Lefleur approached Marley, touched his left shoulder, and just like that they were gone.

22

Chapter 22: Good in Everyone

"I've introduced myself before. But allow me to formally introduce myself to you, you know, with my *real* title and all. I am King Nicklause Jean Lefleur the Third, ruler of the Kingdom of Esseix. I have chosen the greatest soldiers and claimed them as my own, and as you can see, they are quite content here. They have everything they could ever need and want. They don't remember their former lives, so they aren't missing anything." There were a multitude of dungeons in the castle, but there was no need for the boys to be physically confined as the prison was in their minds.

"What did you do? Where are we? Why do you need them?" asked Marley.

"I've simply brought us to my Throne Room so that I can talk to you one on one. Every great king needs an even better army to serve him, young prince. You see for many years —centuries some may say, but time is of no concern to me —I've always known that I was the chosen one. Your father has ruled for far too long. He is a good and kind man, Marley, but what has being good and kind ever gotten anyone but certainty to meet an early demise? What's light without dark? Life needs balance. I am that balance. I am the darkness that everyone so unknowingly but desperately needs. I plan to rule with an iron fist, and I've chosen you to rule alongside me as my prince of darkness. You will have everything you ever wanted and everything you ever needed, if only I can have your loyalty . Unlike the others, I am giving you free will to choose who you will serve. What say you, Marley McGee?"

"You expect me to betray my father, my family, my morals, my values, and all that I know is good and right?" Marley replied.

"*All* of those things are overrated. Every last one of them. Where is your family now when *you* need them? They weren't there for you. They didn't protect you. If they had, you wouldn't be here now, would you? So why are you concerned about betraying them when they first betrayed you. They don't love you. You know that, right, Marley?""No, you're wrong. They do love me. Why have you chosen me to rule by your side? Why are you giving me a choice? Why didn't you just compel me as you did the others?"

"You are special, Prince Marley! I've known this before you were born. You are the next in line for my throne. At first, I perceived you as a threat, but who better to serve as the heir that I never had? I have lived for many, many years. But I won't live forever, and I want my legacy to live on through you."

"I've been through a lot in what I now realize to be a real former life —one of the most significant things being that my father was never in my life," Marley said. "He was never there for any good thing that I accomplished. At times, I've seen my mother and granny do all that they can just to live life and be happy; yet often they were unable to do so, no matter how amazing they were. No matter how good they have been to other people, they could never seem to get ahead until something tragic happened, like my grandfather passing away. Speaking of my grandfather, he was also a kind and good man like King Leigh, my father in this realm, but he died unexpectedly."

"Yes, Marley, now you see what I mean. Now you see that it's pointless to be good," King Lefleur said, becoming excited.

"No, King Lefleur. You didn't let me finish . I was going to say, regardless of all that I have been through and all that I have seen my family go through, I will never choose evil. At times it seems as though the wicked prosper while the good suffer, and that may be true . But in the long run, good always prevails! Always. Now, I'm going to leave and release the other boys so that they can go home to their families." Marley began to walk toward the door.

"How exactly do you think you are going to accomplish that task, Marley? They are happy with their new home. They aren't going anywhere with you."

"No, they are not truly happy. You have them under some sort of spell, and I'll figure out how to free them. Now if you'll excuse me. "

With the evilest of grins on his face, Lefleur asked, "Do you really think I'm going to let you walk out of here just like that, huh? You truly are a naive little boy who sees the best in people —to your own detriment. Just remember you chose your own fate, Prince Marley!"

Lefleur moved his hands together, close to his chest, palms facing forward, and moved them out in front of him in a quick motion causing Marley to hit the ground without ever laying a hand on him.

Marley slowly got up. "No, I didn't think you would let me

leave, but I always try to see the good in people. I thought I'd give you a chance to choose good for a change; but in true form, you chose what you have always chosen."

"Yes, Marley, I am me. Who else would I ever be? The question is— do you know who you are?" King Lefleur motioned at Marley again, pushing him back with a mighty force.

Although Marley went backward, this time, he kept his balance.

"Oh, so you're trying to tap into your inner strength, huh? Well, we'll see about that. You will serve me, one way or another." King Lefleur continued to use his powers to push and restrain Marley with hand motion after hand motion. He never physically touched Marley, but Marley could feel the painful effects of King Lefleur's movements. Each blow upset Marley more and more.

"Enough!" Marley shouted .

As King Lefleur positioned himself to once again strike Marley, Marley grabbed his pendant, held it out toward King Lefleur, and said, *"Debilis potestas!"*

It appeared as though nothing occurred as a result of Marley's chant. King Lefleur laughed and continued with his movement. Marley braced himself for the impact of King Lefleur's blow; but this time nothing happened to Marley. King Lefleur looked surprised and tried again, but still nothing. Marley breathed a sigh of relief, looked at King Lefleur, and walked toward the door to leave and rescue the others.

King Lefleur called to Marley, "What did you do to me, boy? Do you think you're more powerful than me? You're not! I've been around since the beginning of time! I've heard about you! Who you're supposed to be! Who you are! They say you're the savior! But you're not saving anyone!"

King Lefleur ran and retrieved a sword from one of the standing sets of armor in the massive room. "You're not leaving here. Either you serve me, or you serve no one! I will not allow this so-called destiny of yours to be fulfilled. I will never serve you or anyone else! I will reign in absolute power! What say you? Are you with me or against me?"

"I am with my father!" Marley replied.

"Fine, have it your way!" As the last word left his lips, King Lefleur lunged toward Marley with the sword. "Come here, boy!"

Marley retreated, and the blade barely missed him. He retreated farther from Lord Lefleur as he advanced toward him.

"Lord Lefleur, you don't have to do this. I know there is good in you. There is some form of good in everyone."

"Not in me, Marley, not in me."

Lefleur continued to charge at Marley. Marley found himself backing into a corner, then he tripped and fell. He gulped and looked up at the menacing man.

Lefleur walked toward Marley snickering. When he reached him, he stood over him, and with both hands gripping the hilt of his sword, he thrust it down toward Marley with all his might.

23

Chapter 23: Volant a Hic!

The sword's blade was inches away when Marley raised one hand and motioned it toward Lord Lefleur. "*Volant a hic!*" he shouted.

A light shone from Marley's hands, and Lord Lefleur flew across the room. He landed on the floor with a thud and yelled, "Marley McGee!" He angrily got up and ran full speed again charging Marley!

Marley now felt empowered and emboldened! He stood across the room from Lord Lefleur. This time with a sense of calm, Marley closed his eyes. The entire outline of Marley was illuminated. He said with strength, power, and confidence, "*Protero indu alium orbis!*"

Lord Lefleur stopped in his tracks. His sword dropped. "Marley! What did you do?! What's happening to me?!" Lord Lefleur looked at his hands, which were slowly fading. "No, this can't be. You don't have the power to do this to me."

Lord Lefleur was disappearing bit by bit before Marley's eyes. Marley stood there solemnly looking at him disappearing. Marley's heart was pure and good; although Lord Lefleur had tried to hurt him and so many others, Marley took no pleasure in what he had to do. In fact, he had just tapped into another set of powers he didn't know he possessed. He was in a state of shock in addition to being remorseful.As the last of Lord Lefleur faded, he said, "This isn't over, false king. I'll see you again; and sooner than you think, in one form or another."

Then, just like that, there was no trace of him.

Marley gathered himself and ran full speed out of the room and down the hall. He was not certain where he was, but he could hear music playing in the distance. He followed the sound. Shortly thereafter, Marley again heard the voices of boys, but this time, the voices seemed very different.

24

Chapter 24: He Is Who He Says He Is

Marley opened the doors. Whereas before, the boys seemed content, even joyful in their partying, now they were confused and anxious.

"Where am I?"

"Why are we here?"

"How did we get here?"

"What's happening?"

These were all questions that the boys frantically asked.

"Everyone, listen!"

The crowd continued with their questions.

"Everyone, listen up! I am Prince Marley! My friends and I are here to save you! Some of us got here much like you! I don't have time to explain how you got here; but I want to get you home!"

One of the boys responded. "Why are we here Prince Marley?"

Another called out, "Yes, and how do you know anything about how we got here when none of us know anything? How do we know we can trust you?"

"Truth be told, you don't know; but you should trust me! I could've been home living lavishly . My friend had a way for us to leave. We chose to stay as we thought we would be leaving others behind. We absolutely did not want to do that. When we learned you all were here, we did everything in our power to find you. I've done things I didn't know I was capable of to save you. You all have helped me whether you know it or not! Again, we don't have time for me to explain much more at the moment, so I need you to listen."

At that moment, Judah entered the room. He spoke, and the room gasped almost in unison. "Sir! We searched everywhere for you! I believe Lefleur used a concealment spell to hide your location. We circled back around here just in case you came back."

Nakirran and Pierre then entered. They both hurriedly reunited with their brothers, embracing them .

Nakirran then ran to Marley and hugged him. "I'm so glad you're okay."

Marley was pleased.

"Sir, we have to get them out of here," Judah said, interrupting the happy reunion.

"I know, my friend. I just don't know how."

"But you do, my friend. You do. The boys now know who they are; and there's a reason for that. You did that all on your own . You dug deep and outwitted an evil that has been around since the beginning of time. Do what you did then now; but we don't have much time."

Marley again addressed the upset crowd.

"Everyone! I know many of you don't trust that I am who I say I am; but I need you to listen to me. Our lives depend on it. If you want to get back home to your families, I ask that you trust me enough to do as I say."

"He is who he says he is," said Stellan, the young man from Marley's kingdom. He was finally getting back some of his memories. He added, "He is the youngest prince of my kingdom, and I've never known him to be anything less than kind, giving, and brave.""Thank you, Stellan. Now, everyone, all I need for you to do is hold hands, close your eyes, and think of home and those you love. I'll do the rest."

The boys looked at one another, held hands, and closed their eyes. Once Marley saw everyone was linked, he closed his eyes, deeply inhaled, grabbed his pendant, and then slowly exhaled. He opened his eyes and looked around the room at the boys. He felt a sense of responsibility for them. He then made eye contact with Princess Nakirran. She smiled and nodded. Marley clenched his pendant and authoritatively said, *"Reditus domum!"*

Nothing occurred on that first command, but Marley felt in his heart that all would be well.

He called again, *"Reditus domum!"*

The chandelier in the room shook, and some of the furniture was disturbed.

"Reditus domum!"

A bright light shone, and just like that, the grand room was empty.

25

Chapter 25: Gold and Garnets

Marley was back at the tree in his kingdom where Lord Lefleur had tricked him. The young prince was pleased. In that moment, he knew everyone was safely home with their families.

Marley ran to the castle's courtyard, and King Leigh's most loyal soldier, Sir Anthony, spotted him.

"Sir?" he called out. "Prince Marley? Is that you?"

"It is me," Marley replied.

"Sir! Come with me at once! We must report to your father! He's had the entire kingdom searching for you. Follow me! Double time!" The soldier began to run.

"Double time?" Marley muttered . He had no idea what that meant, but he followed the soldier. A group of soldiers followed the two into the castle.

Meanwhile, in the Throne Room, King Leigh sat on his throne with his eyes closed and hands clasped together in deep meditation. He had exhausted all of his resources searching for his son. But he wasn't sitting idly. He sat with purpose. He needed time to gather his thoughts to regroup and make another attempt to find Prince Marley.

The Throne Room guards opened the doors. In ran Sir Anthony with his platoon of soldiers and Prince Marley. King Leigh was still in meditation, and so he did not immediately see his beloved son enter . Soldiers had constantly been in and out of the Throne Room with reports to him, and the king assumed there was nothing special about this visit. He was well protected by his most trusted followers, so he had no reason to be on guard.

Sir Anthony and his soldiers knelt before the king.

"Sir!" Sir Anthony cried out. "We've found the young prince. Your son is home!"

King Leigh opened his eyes and lifted his head. He looked toward the ceiling and humbly said, "Thank you." The kind king looked at the found prince. "Marley, my son. You're back home. Thank you, Sir Anthony, for this gift."

"Sir, humbly, thanks are not due to me," the honest knight replied.

King Leigh arose from his throne. Crowned and clothed in all of his glory, he walked to his son. He embraced him with so much love, and although Marley still had many questions about this new life of his, he was relieved and happy to see his father, the king.

Marley hugged his father and peacefully rested his head on his chest.

King Leigh kissed the top of his son's head and said, "It is well, son. It is well."

Marley replied, "Yes, Father, it is."

King Leigh loved his son dearly. He knew the ability to show that love to his family and the people of his kingdom made him the strong and effective king that he was.

"Sir Anthony!" the king called out with a huge smile. "My trusted soldier and good friend, can you have all of my subjects in the courtyard in an hour? I want the best flowers, decorations, food, beverages, and music that we have there at that time."

"Yes, Your Highness. At once, sir." Sir Anthony stood.

His soldiers stood and exited the Throne Room.

"Marley, I know you've been through a lot. But here you stand before me, tall and strong. Make no mistake, I will address what has happened to you, my boy. But for now, we will celebrate your return. Go to your chamber . I will send someone to assist you with getting prepared for your event tonight. They will dress you in the finest threads and have you well groomed. Your guards have been advised to have you at the Royal Velarium in the courtyard in forty-five minutes. I will notify your brother that you are back. You will see him at the event. I'll see you in a few. "

"Yes, Father," Marley replied.

Marley left his father's Throne Room and walked into the castle's grand halls. The halls were empty as everyone prepared for the celebration of Marley's return. As Marley walked , he thought about everything that had happened and all that he learned he could do. He was grateful for his newfound family, and yes, even his new position and status, but he could not fully enjoy these things. He remembered his mother and grandmother, and he missed them so much.

Soon, Marley was at his chamber. His chamber guards greeted him and opened the massive doors. Marley entered. He looked around and saw none other than his good and loyal friend Judah.

"Judah!" Marley called out .

Then a group of people with a portable wardrobe and

everything that was needed to prepare for the event to celebrate him arrived. "Sir, we have come to prepare you for your gathering," one of them said.

Marley bathed and was dressed in the kingdom's finest threads. He was then crowned with a crown made of gold and garnets. Even Judah's wings were adorned.

"Sir, are you ready?" a guard asked.

Marley nodded with a grin, and the group left for the courtyard.

26

Chapter 26: Home

As Marley walked down the halls to the courtyard with Judah at his side , trumpets majestically sounded. What Marley saw was incredible. The sun was setting, and white flower petals were being thrown into the air by beautiful women dressed in all white. The courtyard's trees and shrubbery were decorated with small white lights. Long wooden tables with large candelabras on them lined the courtyard. As Marley walked toward his father and brother under the Royal Velarium, the massive crowd cheered and chanted his name. The soldiers in the courtyard were called to attention by Sir Anthony for the young leader. King Leigh and David Sebastian stood there waiting to greet Marley.

When Marley reached them, Prince David Sebastian, who stood to his father's left, embraced his brother. King Leigh then embraced his son, grabbed his face, and said, "Job well done, son. Job well done. I'm very proud of you."

King Leigh turned his attention to the formation of soldiers before him. "At ease!" he called out. He then addressed the crowd below. "It is with great pleasure that I hold this event for my youngest son, Prince Marley. As you know, my son, along with another boy from our kingdom, Stellan, was abducted from within our kingdom walls. I want you all to know, evil never prevails. It never has, and it never will. I'm glad to have you both back home. I've been briefed on all that has happened, and I assure you that I am not turning a blind eye to it. But there is a time and place for everything. This moment is the time for us to celebrate the safe return not only of my son but of Stellan and many other boys from other kingdoms. It is time to rejoice in the bravery of my son, who served so selflessly, saving the futures of many young men, and might I add, a princess of one of our ally kingdoms. I thank you all for gracing us with your presence. Please enjoy the food and festivities and have a good night."

The night was magical. There was not a face present without a smile. Everyone danced and indulged in the kingdom's finest food and drinks. They laughed at the court jesters and sang their merry hearts away. Prince Marley especially enjoyed his time with his father and brother. Marley had never felt this fatherly love. It was different, it was new, but it was good. Marley also never knew what it felt like to have a sibling. He had always been an only child. He enjoyed the camaraderie that having a brother provided him. Although David Sebastian had gotten onto Marley a few times, Marley felt it came from a place of love and concern.

Marley hadn't spent much time with them, but being with them felt right. For once, while in the kingdom, Marley decided to stop asking questions about why he was there. He could never and would never forget or forsake his mother and grandmother, but the new prince decided if he was going to live in Savagna, he would embrace his new family. Prince Marley

McGee would embrace his new home.

When the event was over, Marley and David Sebastian, accompanied by their guards, headed back to their chambers. They walked and talked, laughing about their night. The brothers were happy. They reached Marley's room first.

"All right, little brother, no shenanigans tonight. Stay in your room and out of trouble. Understood?" David Sebastian broke the serious expression on his face with a grin. "Give me a hug, little brother. I love you, and I'm very proud of you." David Sebastian patted Marley on the back and then retired to his chamber.

Then Marley bid his guards good night and prepared for bed.

The prince was now at peace as he lay in bed. And Judah, just like on Marley's first night in the castle, was by his friend's side on the floor .

"Job well done, sir. Get some rest."

"You, too, friend. Thank you for everything."

Marley looked over and saw that Judah had quickly fallen asleep. Marley then turned his head and looked out his window at the beautiful night sky. A full moon shone bright, and the countless stars looked like tiny fireflies . Marley gazed at the stars. His eyes began to get heavy, and soon he had fallen asleep.

27

Chapter 27: The Voice

"Marley!"

Marley abruptly sat up from his sleep, breathing heavily.

"Mom?" he uttered . Marley looked around. It was still dark.

"Judah?" he whispered. Marley couldn't see a thing. He touched his face. His sleep mask was on. Marley removed the mask and saw that he was back in his grandfather's —well, that he was back in his home. It was still night, and just as at the palace, Marley could see the moon and the stars from his window. They illuminated his room.

"I must've been dreaming," he said. "I knew it."

Marley lay back down. Having forgotten that his mom had called him, he closed his eyes and began to doze off again.

Thud!

Marley quickly sat up. He had heard something fall in his room. Marley looked around and didn't see anything on the floor, and so he lay back down.

Boom!

Marley again sat up.

Boom!

He looked around and again saw nothing.

Boom!

Marley soon realized the noises were coming from his closet. Frightened, he sat there, too afraid to leave his bed. Marley knew he no longer possessed the powers that he had in Savagna. He was again just an average boy. The time between the noises decreased, and soon the sounds were rapidly occurring one after the other.

Boom! Boom! Boom! Boom!

Marley sat there staring at the door. He grabbed his pendant. His eyes were big with fear, and his chest rapidly rose and fell with deep and panicked breaths. The thunderous knocks on the closet door continued. Then, all of a sudden, the noises ceased!

Marley wiped the sweat from his forehead and waited to see if the noises would return. They didn't. He got up and slowly walked to his closet door. Marley cautiously turned the handle. He gulped, closed his eyes, then opened them, and pulled the door open with force.

"Who's there?" Marley called out.

At that very moment, Marley's bedroom door opened, and his light turned on.

"Marley!"

Marley screamed and turned toward his door.

"Mom," he said, panting. "You frightened me!"

"I frightened you? Um. Okay, baby boy. I apologize. I heard noises in here and was just making sure you were okay. I just got home from work. Are you okay in here?"

Marley closed the closet door and walked to his mom. "Yes, Mom. I'm okay. I love you." Marley hugged his mom.

"I love you too. Since when did you start saying *frightened* ? And why are you speaking with an accent? Get some rest, baby boy. It seems you need it."

"Yes, ma'am. I will. Good night."

"Good night, Marley." Marley's mom turned his light off, closed his door, and headed to her room.

Marley got back in bed and pulled the covers over him. As he began to lie back down, he saw through the crack at the bottom of the closet door that the light was turned on. An otherworldly voice called out from it. "Marley!"

The prince sat up and screamed, "Judaahhhhhh!"

About the Author

K. E. Argrow is an imaginative author who first wrote a book in the third grade. Although, since then, the writer has written many works to include poetry, song lyrics, and children's books, *Marley McGee the Majestic* is the author's first published work. The magical writer is an Army Veteran and Master of Business Administration (MBA) holder.

You can connect with me on:

https://www.marleyenterprisesllc.com